GOOD D🐾G

Barnyard Buddies

by
Cam Higgins

illustrated by
Ariel Landy

LITTLE SIMON

New York London Toronto Sydney New Delhi

LITTLE SIMON

An imprint of Simon & Schuster Children's Publishing Division

1230 Avenue of the Americas, New York, New York 10020

First Little Simon hardcover edition February 2022

Copyright © 2022 by Simon & Schuster, Inc.

Also available in a Little Simon paperback edition.

All rights reserved, including the right of reproduction in whole or in part in any form. LITTLE SIMON is a registered trademark of Simon & Schuster, Inc., and associated colophon is a trademark of Simon & Schuster, Inc.

For information about special discounts for bulk purchases, please contact Simon & Schuster Special Sales at 1-866-506-1949 or business@simonandschuster.com.

The Simon & Schuster Speakers Bureau can bring authors to your live event. For more information or to book an event contact the Simon & Schuster Speakers Bureau at 1-866-248-3049 or visit our website at www.simonspeakers.com.

Designed by Leslie Mechanic

Manufactured in the United States of America 1221 FFG

10 9 8 7 6 5 4 3 2 1

Library of Congress Cataloging-in-Publication Data

Names: Higgins, Cam, author. | Landy, Ariel, illustrator.

Title: Barnyard buddies / by Cam Higgins ; illustrated by Ariel Landy.

Description: First Little Simon edition. | New York: Little Simon, 2022. | Series: Good dog ; #7 | Audience: Ages 5–9.

Summary: Farm puppy Bo feels left out and jealous when his best friend Scrapper comes to visit.

Identifiers: LCCN 2021044178 (print) | LCCN 2021044179 (ebook) | ISBN 9781665905886 (paperback) | ISBN 9781665905893 (hardcover) | ISBN 9781665905909 (ebook)

Subjects: CYAC: Dogs—Fiction. | Animals—Infancy—Fiction. | Best friends—Fiction. | Friendship—Fiction. | Jealousy—Fiction. | Farm life—Fiction.

Classification: LCC PZ7.1.H54497 Bar 2022 (print) | LCC PZ7.1.H54497 (ebook) | DDC [E]—dc23

LC record available at https://lccn.loc.gov/2021044178

CONTENTS

So Many Farm Friends

I love being a farm pup. There are so many animals to play with, and I'm lucky to have lots of friends! Take my good buddy Zonks, for example.

He's my pig pal, and his pigpen has the best mud on the farm. My favorite thing about him is that Zonks is always down to play roll-in-the-mud.

Pigs and mud go together like peanut butter and jelly, milk and cookies, or spaghetti and meatballs.

I love playing in the squishy mud too, of course. But for some reason my humans are never very happy with me afterward.

Whenever I come home after playing with Zonks, Darnell, my human dad, lets out a big sigh and rushes me to the bath every single time!

Then there's my friend Comet the
foal. I can always count on Comet
for a race around the farm. Horses
are very strong, and they have really
long legs, so it's not easy to keep up
with her, except if we're playing fetch.

When it comes to fetch, I can run for miles. But if we're racing for fun, I usually just want to curl up for a nap after.

The baby chicks, ducks, and sheep, who are all so fluffy and kind, are my friends too.

Seeing them always brightens my day. We play all sorts of games, like hide-and-go-sheep and duck-duck-goose, out in the grassy meadow.

The chicks are faster than you'd think and are almost too good at hiding. They can fit into places that are way too small for a dog like me.

Then, of course, last but not least, there are the barn cats, King and Diva. While they're far from the friendliest cats you'll ever meet, even *they* make the farm feel busy and full of life.

Now, it can get crazy sometimes. But the more animals there are on the farm, the more fun there is to be had. And so I always say, the more the merrier!

Scrapper's Visit

I was thinking about how awesome it is to live here when all of a sudden, my best buddy, Scrapper, appeared in front of me. It was my lucky day!

Scrapper lives on the farm nearby. And I swear, it was like he read my mind—nothing makes me happier than hanging out with my best friend.

"Scrapper! You're just the dog I wanted to see! How did you know I wanted to play?" I yelped.

"Hey, Bo! How are ya?" Scrapper barked back as he ran around in a happy circle. "I just went for a run in the field. It's so hot today, isn't it?"

Scrapper and I always have the most fun adventures in the forest. We like to hunt for monsters and dig holes together. And we really are the best of friends—the kind who will chase after squirrels for each other.

"Yeah, it's way too hot to be outside," I panted. "I'm not sure what we can pla—"

But before I could even finish my thought, Scrapper ran past me and headed straight toward the pigpen.

"Hey! Where are you going?" I called.

I eagerly followed, but when we got to the pigpen, I stopped short. I blinked three times, but my eyes weren't playing tricks on me. Scrapper and Zonks were definitely playing a game of roll-in-the-mud together.

Without me. And I didn't even know they were friends!

"Oh, hi, Bo!" Zonks oinked.

"Hey, Zonks," I said after a pause. "You two know each other?"

"We sure do!" Scrapper piped in. "Zonks's pigpen has the best mud for a hot, sunny day!"

"Um, yeah, you're right," I agreed.
"I didn't know you knew."

Now, on any other ordinary day,
I would have jumped right in. Like
Scrapper said, nothing beats playing in
the cool, cool mud on a hot day.

Well, except for maybe digging in the dirt for bones. Oh, and chewing on socks. The really smelly socks that I sometimes find under the couch are the best. And then there's waiting for yummy scraps under the dinner table. Yeah, I love that too.

But other than that, on a hot summer day, playing in wet, squishy mud would be my idea of fun. Except . . . today felt different.

As I watched Zonks and Scrapper rolling, chasing, and laughing together, suddenly a strange, tickly feeling started bubbling up in my tummy.

Oh, no, I didn't feel good at all. Did I eat something bad for breakfast?

I don't think I've ever said no to a mud playdate. But I knew that getting dirty was probably not the best medicine for an upset stomach.

So, before Scrapper or Zonks looked up, I quietly slipped out of the pigpen to find something else to do.

Animals
Need Animals

My favorite thing about farm life is that all the animals are like one big family. But I never would have guessed that one of my barnyard friends might also know my pal Scrapper.

I wasn't upset about it, but I was a bit confused. Friends should share everything, shouldn't they?

I was so busy wondering about all the questions I had that my head started to feel a little light and dizzy.

Wyatt and Imani, my human brother
and sister, were in the stable, and I
almost bumped into them!

"Hey, Bo!" Wyatt called out. "I was wondering where you were. Want to give me a hand?"

I let out a bark to say *thanks, but no thanks.* I was on a mission to find a barnyard buddy to play with.

So I walked right past Wyatt and jumped into Comet's stall.

Rain or shine, I'm used to finding Comet in the same place. But today, her stall was empty. I couldn't believe it!

"Bo! Come here, boy!" Imani yelled. "Come on, Bo, outta there!" I perked up at Imani's voice.

She sounded upset with me, but I had no idea why. I slunk out of Comet's stall, my tail between my legs.

All I wanted was to find a friend to play with, but no one seemed to care to have me around today.

For the first time ever, a tiny thought popped into my head. What if I didn't have many barnyard buddies after all?

There's Comet!

I decided to head out to the big open field, where I know Comet likes to run. When I run, I usually like to chase after a ball, a long stick, or a stinky (yummy) sock—or even after my own tail!

But Comet taught me that you don't always have to chase something to enjoy the feeling of moving your body.

Sometimes, running just to feel the air rush through your fur and whistle past your ears feels great too.

That's another thing I love about farm life—all the animals here share the same home, but we all like different things and are one of a kind.

This means that I always learn from my friends. Being pals with an animal who's so much bigger than me is so much fun . . . and always interesting!

As I reached the big field, I spotted Comet galloping around in a wide circle. *I knew it. There she is!* I thought. I ran at top speed to catch up to her.

But as I drew closer, I saw two other animals chasing Comet. It was none other than Zonks and Scrapper!

I slowed down, not sure if I should bother them. But that's when Scrapper saw me.

"Hi, Bo!" Scrapper yipped. "Comet is showing us the jumps she's been practicing. Look how high she can go!"

I watched as Comet galloped down the field and jumped over a white rail. Scrapper woofed with excitement, and Zonks oinked with awe.

"Way to go, Comet!" they cheered. "That was awesome!"

I barked too. Comet's jump was very impressive. I couldn't believe it!

But as I watched Zonks and Scrapper run over to Comet to congratulate her, my stomach started to not feel so good. Was I really getting sick?

I walked over to my three friends. "Nice jump, Comet," I said softly.

Before Comet could say anything, Scrapper had an idea. "Hey! I know what we should do! We should all head over to the swimming hole and cool off in the water."

My heart gave a little flutter of
excitement—I loved going to the
swimming hole!

But then I remembered something important. "Oh, but Comet doesn't like to get wet," I told Scrapper. "Horses don't play in the water the way dogs do."

I was certain that I knew Comet better than anyone else. She was *my* friend, after all.

But to my surprise, Comet piped up. "Oooh, the swimming hole sounds like fun! Let's go!"

I looked up to ask Comet if she was sure, but my friends were already walking away. So I ignored the strange feeling in my tummy and ran to catch up.

To the Swimming Hole

Since it was Scrapper's idea to go to the swimming hole, he happily led us toward the lake. Scrapper loves the water. He's the friend who helped me get over my own fear and finally learn to swim.

But I didn't understand how he could be so sure of where to go.

Scrapper didn't live here on the Davis farm. He was used to walking to the swimming hole from his own home next door—from the other direction.

If anyone knew their way around the Davis farm, it was me. But I didn't want to hurt Scrapper's feelings, so I stayed quiet. I hung back behind Zonks as we crossed the field.

Soon we came to the big rock
where I was sure we had to turn left.
But Scrapper led us to the right!

My nose always knows where to go;
it has never once steered me wrong.

And my nose was telling me to go left.
I knew Scrapper also used his nose,
just like I did. And his nose was telling
him to go in the opposite direction.

I always thought I knew Scrapper best. After all, dogs know dogs best. But I wasn't sure if I could trust his nose over mine. What if following Scrapper's nose led us in circles? Or worse—what if we got lost?

I was sure that we would end up in a part of the forest we shouldn't be in. But within a few minutes, Scrapper led us to a clearing where the lake glimmered. My mouth dropped open. How did Scrapper know his way around *my* farm?

"Wow! Nice going, Scrapper!" Zonks oinked. "You sure got us to the watering hole fast. Come on, let's jump in!"

Zonks and Scrapper raced to the lake's edge, both squealing with glee as they dove into the water.

I had no idea pigs loved water as much as they loved mud! I turned to look for Comet. She had a horsey grin as she watched her reflection rippling on the water's surface.

"Wow, it's so pretty here," she whinnied. "This was a great idea, Scrapper!"

As I watched my friends enjoy the water, a part of me was super happy. But it was getting harder to ignore that weird feeling in my stomach. It felt like a frog was jumping around my tummy, and I didn't know what to do!

Scrapper
to the Rescue!

I love swimming, so an upset stomach wasn't going to stop me. I took a deep breath and jumped in. The water welcomed me like a cool hug. My body relaxed as I paddled along.

Luckily, my tummy felt better right away! I happily doggy-paddled over to Scrapper and Zonks.

"Watch me, everybody!" I jumped out of the water and trotted a few paces away. Then I ran toward the watering hole as fast as I could. I landed on my belly with a loud *smack*.

"Hooray, Bo!" barked Scrapper.

"Nice belly flop!" Zonks oinked.

I shook my fur, sending a flurry of water droplets into the air. I floated on my tummy and enjoyed the feeling of the warm sunshine on my back. Everything felt peaceful for the first time all afternoon.

Zonks paddled over to Comet to keep her company. "Hey, Comet," he said. "Why don't you come into the water with us?"

Comet neighed nervously. "I don't know, Zonks. I don't swim. This water looks very deep."

"You don't have to go swimming. Just take a few steps in—it'll feel nice on your hooves," Zonks said.

"Well, looking at the water is great, but being *in* the water is different."

My ears perked up. I knew all we needed to do was help her feel comfortable.

"Hey, Comet, it's okay—just take it one step at a time," I said.

So with everyone's eyes on her, she swished her tail and slowly put one hoof in the water.

"That's it!" I called excitedly. "You're doing it!"

Slowly but surely, she took another step and waded a bit farther into the lake. Soon, she had all four legs in the water.

"Woo-hoo! You did it, Comet!" I barked. I eagerly splashed the water with my tail.

But as we were horsing around, a small river rock got kicked into the air and plopped down and hit Comet in the face. Comet reared back with a loud *NEIGH*.

"Oh, Comet, I'm so sorry!" I yelled, swimming over. But my paddling just splashed more water her way! She was running around so much that I lost my balance and fell back into the water with a loud *SPLASH*.

I couldn't believe it. Things just went from bad to worse. And that's when Scrapper stepped in.

WOOF, WOOF! Scrapper barked loudly. Scrapper knew that all he needed to do was remind Comet that she wasn't in danger. And it worked!

Before we knew it, Comet calmed down and was back on dry land.

I was so relieved that Comet was okay. My friends were happily playing again too, but my upset tummy was back. So I quietly slipped away to head home.

Cats Got
Your Tongue

As I was walking back through the forest, I suddenly got a weird feeling, like I was being watched. My doggy senses were on high alert, so I looked around and chased after my own tail.

And then I saw it. Two sets of golden eyes were staring at me from within the green bushes.

75

Of course, it was just my luck that
I'd bump into the barnyard cats, King
and Diva, at a not-so-great time.

76

"Hey, why the big pout? Cats got your tongue, puppy?" Diva hissed. Then she let out a snarky laugh as she circled around me.

"Aw, please, just leave me alone," I woofed, trying my best to ignore them.

"It certainly seems like all your little barnyard buddies are willing to leave you alone," King said slyly. "Especially after you scared poor Comet."

I already felt so bad for frightening Comet. And these cats were not helping one bit.

"Don't you have anything better to do than make fun of me?" I growled.

"Aw, lighten up. We just happened to have the good luck of being in the right place at the right time to spy your big boo-boo."

"Yeah, right," I grumbled.

"Poor Bo. We should go easy on him. After today, there might just be a new favorite dog on the farm," Diva said with a sneaky laugh.

I had to admit—these cats really knew how to get into my head. But I couldn't let them get to me, so I darted ahead of them, back toward the house.

Soon, the sound of their laughter grew softer. But their words kept echoing in my head. What if they were right? What if everyone liked Scrapper better than they liked me?

A New Dog Hero on the Farm?

When I finally got back to the farm, I headed past the chicken coop on my way to the house. I could hear the chicks chirping busily.

"Why, hello, Bo!" they cried excitedly, just like they always do. I was thankful that even on a not-so-great day, there were some things that didn't change.

Penny, a fluffy yellow chick, hopped over to me. "Hey, Bo, Scrapper is your best dog friend, right?" she tweeted.

I nodded. "Uh-huh. How do you know Scrapper?" I asked.

"Oh, you're so lucky to have such a good friend! He came by earlier and helped us dig eggs out of the coop. King and Diva had tried to play hide-and-seek with us . . . by burying the eggs."

"That's nice," I said softly. I knew they were right. Scrapper was a great pup, and anyone would want to be friends with him. I loved being his friend, but today, I felt totally unlucky.

The strange ticklish feeling in my tummy was stronger than ever. But now the bubbly feeling had risen up like it was stuck in my throat. Would barking make it come out?

I said good-bye to the chicks and
continued to the field, where Nanny
Sheep and her flock were grazing.

Turns out that *they* were over the moon and couldn't stop baaing about Scrapper too!

Everywhere I turned, the animals were talking about Scrapper—how great he was at finding lost things, making up fun games, *and* helping out.

Today was supposed to be the most fun-filled day, but it totally hadn't gone my way.

All my barnyard friends were busy buzzing about how wonderful Scrapper was.

I couldn't believe it, but for the first time ever, I wished Scrapper hadn't come over at all.

9

A
Heart-to-Heart

Just as I was thinking about him, I saw Scrapper running toward me.

"Hey, Bo!" Scrapper barked happily. "I'm so glad you're here! Comet and Zonks and I have been looking for you!"

Zonks and Comet came up behind Scrapper. "Heya, Bo! There you are. We've been searching for you for ages!"

I was so confused. My friends were happy to see . . . *me*?

"I had lots of fun playing in the water with you," I said, turning to look at Comet. "And I'm so happy you enjoyed the water too. I know how scary it can seem at first."

Comet neighed joyfully. "Yes, it was wonderful! And what helped me feel more comfortable was having my good friends, like you, with me."

I broke into a big doggy smile. Suddenly the lump in my throat got smaller, but the tickly feeling in my tummy was still there.

Zonks and Comet happily headed back toward the barn. But Scrapper stayed by my side.

"Bo?" he asked. "What's wrong? I can tell something's up."

Wow, see what I mean? Pups sure do know pups best.

I hung my head and finally decided to let it out.

"When all my barnyard friends wanted to play with you, I guess I started to feel a little . . . left out."

"Aw, Bo," Scrapper said. "We didn't mean to make you feel bad."

"Well, it was also that I felt kind of jealous. You're so good at helping all the animals—like with Comet in the lake, and the chicks with their eggs. You even knew how to find the watering hole from *our* farm! How did you do that so fast?"

"Oh, that was nothing," Scrapper barked. "I followed a flock of ducks I spotted in the sky! It was pure luck that I found a shortcut."

"See? You're so good at everything, Scrapper!" I told my friend.

"Well, all dogs are good at finding lost things—you are too! And I was able to help Comet calm down thanks to you. I knew how to help her feel less scared of the water because I had already helped you before."

"Wow, thanks. That makes sense," I said.

"But I'm really sorry I made you feel left out," Scrapper said. "I was just so excited to have all these new friends."

"I'm sorry too," I replied. "All of us are lucky to have you for a friend. And I'm so glad you came over to play!"

One
Big Family

After that, for the first time all day, the weird ticklish feeling in my stomach was all gone.

Everyone was back on the farm, and it finally felt like everything was as it should be. I was so focused on what I thought my friends thought that I didn't really get to have much fun.

Now the day was already over, and the sun was close to setting. This meant it was just about time for Scrapper to head back home.

Because no dog wants to miss dinnertime. Dinner is when humans give out the best scraps from under the table.

Luckily, the sun decided to linger
in the evening sky just long enough
for all of us to play a few more games.

This time, Comet, Zonks, the chicks, Scrapper, and I all played together. The more friends there were, the better!

Scrapper and I played roll-in-the-mud with Zonks, then we raced Comet around the field, and then we helped the chicks dig for worms. It was so much fun!

At the end, Scrapper and I rolled onto our backs. There is nothing quite like looking up at a summer night's sky.

We watched as the sun went to bed
and the sky was streaked with pink,
purple, and orange.

In that moment, I realized that even if we get upset or misunderstand one another sometimes, we barnyard animals are one big family. No matter what.

And the great news was that we could make room for one more. My best dog buddy, Scrapper, would always be welcome to join all of us for some barnyard fun!

Here's a peek at Bo's next big adventure!

GOOD D🐾G 8

Puppy Luck

The sun was shining brightly in the sky. Glimmers of golden light fell across the fields and trees. What a beautiful day!

And it was an exciting day too. I was so happy for Clucks the hen, Rufus the rooster, and all the chicks. Their coop was getting a brand-new paint job!

An excerpt from *Puppy Luck*

Jennica and Darnell, my human parents, made the design, and Imani and Wyatt, my human sister and brother, were going to help paint. They had all the tools they needed—paint, brushes, rollers, and pans. Everything was lined up on a large piece of tarp.

"We're going to paint the coop red— to match the barn," Jennica explained to the kids. "And we'll give it a nice white trim, too."

All the animals watched as Darnell brushed the first stroke of bright red paint over the wood panel. Clucks pecked at the ground excitedly.

An excerpt from *Puppy Luck*

"Oooh, I can't wait to see what our new home looks like!" she cried. "Rufus, aren't you thrilled too?"

Rufus strutted past, a bored look on his face.

"Sure, sure, although it isn't exactly a new coop," he crowed. He clearly was not anywhere near as amused as Clucks was.

"Yes, but the new red color will make it feel like new!" she replied.

An excerpt from *Puppy Luck*